PUFFIN

D0510075

The Swoose

Dick King-Smith served in the Grenadier Guards during the Second World War, and afterwards spent twenty years as a farmer in Gloucestershire, the county of his birth. Many of his stories are inspired by his farming experiences. Later he taught at a village primary school. His first book, *The Fox Busters*, was published in 1978. Since then he has written a great number of children's books, including *The Sheep-Pig* (winner of the *Guardian* Award and filmed as *Babe*), *Harry's Mad*, *Noah's Brother*, *The Hodgeheg*, *Martin's Mice*, *Ace*, *The Cuckoo Child* and *Harriet's Hare* (winner of the Children's Book Award in 1995). At the British Book Awards in 1992 he was voted Children's Author of the Year. He is married, with three children and eleven grandchildren, and lives in a seventeenth-century cottage a short crow's-flight from the house where he was born.

Dick King-Smith

The Swoose

Illustrated by Judy Brown

PUFFIN BOOKS

PUFFIN BOOKS

Published by the Penguin Group
Penguin Books Ltd, 27 Wrights Lane, London W8 5TZ, England
Penguin Putnam Inc., 375 Hudson Street, New York,
New York 10014, USA
Penguin Books Australia Ltd, Ringwood, Victoria, Australia
Penguin Books Canada Ltd, 10 Alcorn Avenue, Toronto,
Ontario, Canada M4V 3B2
Penguin Books (NZ) Ltd, Private Bag 102902, NSMC,
Auckland, New Zealand

On the worldwide web at: www.penguin.com

Penguin Books Ltd, Registered Offices: Harmondsworth,
Middlesex, England

First published by Viking 1993
Published in Puffin Books 1994
3 5 7 9 10 8 6 4 2

Set inPalatino

Made and printed in England by Clays Ltd, St Ives plc

British Library Cataloguing in Publication Data
A CIP catalogue record for this book is available from
the British Library

ISBN 0–140–34960–X

1.

"Mum," said Fitzherbert. "Why do I look different from all the other goslings on the farm?"

He did, there was no denying it. He was larger than the rest, his feet were bigger, and his neck was longer.

"You *are* different," said his mother.

"Because I'm an only child, d'you mean?"

The other geese all had five or six goslings apiece, but Fitzherbert alone had hatched from his mother's clutch of eggs.

"An only child in more ways than one," she said. "I doubt if there's another bird like you in the whole wide world. All these other youngsters will grow up to be ordinary common or garden geese, but not you, Fitzherbert my boy."

"But I'm a goose like you, Mum, aren't I?" said Fitzherbert.

"No," said his mother, "you are not." She lowered her voice.

"You," she said softly, "are a swoose."

Fitzherbert coiled his long neck backwards into the shape of an S.

"A what?" he cried.

"Ssssssssh!" hissed his mother, and she waddled off to a distant corner of the

farmyard, away from all the other geese.

Fitzherbert hurried after her.

"What did you say I was?" he asked.

His mother looked around to make sure they were out of earshot of the rest of the flock, and then she said, "Now listen carefully. What I am about to tell you must be a secret between you and me, always. D'you understand?"

"Yes, Mum," said Fitzherbert.

"You are old enough now to be told," said his mother, "why you are unlike all the other goslings on the farm. They are the children of a number of geese, but all of them have the same father."

"The old grey gander, you mean?"

"Yes."

"But isn't he my father too?"

"No."

"Then who is?"

"Your father," said Fitzherbert's mum, and a dreamy look came over her face as she spoke, "is neither old nor grey. Your father is young and strong and as white as the driven snow. Never shall I forget the day we met!"

"Where was that, Mum?"

"It was by the river. I had gone down by myself for a swim, when suddenly he appeared, high in the sky above. Oh, the music of his great wings! It was love at first flight! Then he landed on the surface in a shower of spray and swam towards me."

"But I don't get it, Mum," said Fitzherbert. "What was he? Another sort of goose?"

"No," said his mother. "He was a swan."

"What's that?"

"A swan is the most beautiful of all

birds, and your father was the most
beautiful of all swans."

"What was his name?"

"He didn't say. He was a mute swan."

Fitzherbert thought about all this for a
while.

Then he said, "So I might be the only
swoose in the world?"

"Yes."

12

"There aren't any other swooses?"

"Sweese."

"Eh?"

"When there's more than one goose, you say geese. So more than one swoose would be sweese."

"But there isn't more than one. Just me. You just said so, didn't you?"

As mothers do, Fitzherbert's mum

became fed up with his constant questions.

"Oh, run away and play," she said.

But playing with the other goslings wasn't a lot of fun for Fitzherbert. Already they had noticed that he was different. They poked fun at him, calling him Bigfeet or Snakyneck, and they wouldn't let him join in their games.

Time passed, and Fitzherbert began to grow his adult feathers. Often, as he thought of his father swooping down from the sky on whistling wings, he flapped his own and wished that he too could fly. Farmyard geese like his mother and the rest couldn't, he knew – they were too heavy-bodied to get off the ground. But swans could. How about a swoose? And the more he thought about his father, the more he wanted to meet

him. So one day he decided to go down to the river by himself. He would say nothing to his mother about it, but just set off when she wasn't looking.

He had never before been out of the farmyard, and he was not at all sure what the river looked like, let alone where it was, but luck was on his side. He walked across a couple of fields and there it was, in front of him!

Fitzherbert looked at the wide stretch of water, winking and gleaming in the sunlight and chuckling to itself as it flowed along. Never in his life had he swum upon anything but the duckpond at the farm, but this – this is the place for swimming, he thought, and he waddled down the bank and pushed off.

He paddled about in midstream, looking up at the sky, hoping that a snow-white shape would come gliding down to greet him.

Instead he suddenly turned to see a whole armada of snow-white shapes sailing silently downstream towards him. There must have been at least twenty swans, all making for this stranger who dared to swim upon their river. Their wings were curved in excitement, and the look in their black eyes was far from friendly.

Oh, thought Fitzherbert, as the fleet of swans approached, all now grunting and hissing angrily, oh dear, I really must fly!

2.

As Fitzherbert swam hastily away from
his pursuers, he spread his wings and
beat them madly on the water in an
effort to increase his speed. Harder and
harder he flapped, and then he felt his
body lift a little so that now, instead of
swimming, he was slapping his broad
webs on the surface in a kind of clumsy
run.

Suddenly he was airborne, and the swans, satisfied that they had seen off the stranger, did not trouble to follow.

It wasn't much of a flight, that first effort. For perhaps a quarter of a mile, Fitzherbert laboured along only a few yards above the water, and then, tired out by his efforts, flopped back down into the river. He looked anxiously around, but to his great relief, there was no sign of the swans. Nasty, bad-tempered creatures, he said to himself. I wasn't doing them any harm. Why, my dad might have been one of that lot. I don't know that I want to meet him after all.

He swam on, looking about him with interest. He could see other birds on the water – different sorts of duck, and moorhen, and coot – and there was a sudden brilliant flash of colour as a

kingfisher darted across. There were
people on the river too, in rowing-boats
and punts, and one very long thin craft
shot by with eight large young men
pulling at their oars, while a ninth much
smaller man steered and shouted at them
through a kind of tube held to his
mouth.

"In! Out! In! Out!" he called, and the blades dipped and rose as one.

Fitzherbert drifted dreamily with the current, enjoying the sunlit scene, when suddenly a sharp voice cried, "Avast there, you landlubber, or you'll run us down!"

Startled, the swoose looked down to meet the angry gaze of a small water-vole.

"Oh sorry!" said Fitzherbert. "I'm afraid I wasn't looking where I was going."

The vole did not answer, but swam to the bank. Fitzherbert followed.

"I suppose you couldn't tell me?" he said.

The vole turned at the mouth of his burrow.

"Tell you what?" he said.

"Where I'm going?"

23

The vole stared beadily at the swoose.

"Are you feather-brained?" he said.

"No, I'm Fitzherbert."

The water-vole shook his blunt head as though to clear it.

"Tell us something," he said. "You come sailing along without any regard

for the rule of the river, and then you go
and talk a load of rubbish. Anyways, I
never in my life set eyes on a bird like
you before. What are you?"

"I'm a . . . " began Fitzherbert, and
then he thought, oh no, I promised Mum
I wouldn't tell.

"I can't really say," he replied.

"You don't know what you are," said
the vole. "You don't know where you're
going. Next thing, you'll be telling me
you don't know what river this is."

"No. I don't."

"Then you don't know the name of
that town you can see, down at the end
of the reach?"

"No."

"Nor the castle on the hill above it?"

"No."

"Nor who lives in that castle?"

"No," said Fitzherbert. "I've never

been outside our farmyard before. But I'd be very grateful if you'd tell me."

"You're lucky, young fellow," said the vole. "You've come to the right chap. Now, if you'd asked a moorhen, or worse, a duck, you'd have been wasting your breath. But there isn't much that I don't know about this here stretch of the Thames."

"The what?"

"The Thames. That's the name of this river. Most famous river in all England, I'd say. And that town yonder is Windsor, and that's Windsor Castle above it. Now then, surely you know who lives there?"

"No."

"Why, the Queen, of course."

"Oh," said Fitzherbert. "What's a queen?" he said.

The water-vole sighed deeply.

"You're a bright one," he said. "She's only the most important person in the land, that's all."

At this point a pair of swans appeared in midstream.

Fitzherbert backed into a clump of reeds and kept his head down.

"Now d'you see those swans?" said the vole. "They belong to the Queen, they do, like every other swan in the country. Royal birds, swans are."

28

Oh, thought Fitzherbert, I wonder if sweese are? I bet she's never seen one.

"This queen," he said. "What's she called?"

"Victoria. She's been Queen for donkey's years, she has."

"Donkey's ears?" said Fitzherbert.

"Why, 'tis ages ago she lost her husband."

"Couldn't she find him again?"

The water-vole sighed and continued.

"And ever since she's shut herself up in that castle. Always dressed in black, she is. The Widow of Windsor, they call her."

"How do you know all these things?" asked Fitzherbert.

"I keep my ears open," said the water-vole. "Windsor folk come out boating on the river and I listen to all the latest gossip."

"She doesn't sound very happy, this queen," said Fitzherbert.

"She isn't. Grumpy old thing, from all accounts."

"Perhaps she needs cheering up."

"Easier said than done. Anybody tries making a joke, she says, 'We are not amused'," said the vole, and with that he vanished into his burrow.

A moment later he stuck his head out again.

"She might be amused at you," he
said. "Why don't you pay her a visit?"

Why don't I? thought the swoose.

"I will," he said, "and I'll come back
and tell you all about it."

Then it occurred to him that there were
probably a great many water-voles living
beside the Thames.

"So can you tell me your name,
please?" he said.

"Alph," said the vole, and he
disappeared once more.

3.

Dressed all in black, Queen Victoria
stood at an upper window in Windsor
Castle and looked down at the courtyard
below. In the centre of this courtyard
was a perfect square of brilliantly green
grass, a lawn that was not only
personally mown by the Royal Head
Gardener, but afterwards finely

manicured by a number of under-gardeners. No other feet were allowed upon this lawn, save those of the Queen's pet dogs and of the footman who tidied up after them with an elegant brass shovel.

But now it seemed there was a large shape, right in the centre of the square of green.

The Queen held out a hand.

"Our pince-nez," she said to her Lady of the Bedchamber, and when these were brought, she fitted them upon the bridge of the Royal nose.

For some moments she stared down, and then she said, "And what, pray, is that?"

"It is a bird, ma'am," said the Lady of the Bedchamber.

"We can see that," said Queen Victoria. "We are not blind. See that it is

removed immediately. Whatever is it doing on our grass?" and she turned away from the window.

The Lady of the Bedchamber heaved a sigh of relief that she'd avoided having to answer the Queen's last question. She could see plainly what the bird had that moment done on the grass.

"That's better!" said Fitzherbert as he waddled away from the large squelchy mess he had just made.

He was feeling pretty pleased with himself. Everything had gone swimmingly. He had swum on down the Thames, keeping well away from swans, and stopping every now and then to feed on juicy water-plants. It was late in the day before he came to the town, so he decided to wait till next morning before visiting the castle.

At dawn Fitzherbert looked up to see its looming walls and towers. Good job sweese can fly, he thought, and he took off and flew up the hill.

The town of Windsor was still asleep and its streets were as yet empty of the busy horse-drawn traffic. Only a

milkman driving his cart with its load of
brass-bound wooden churns noticed a
large bird fly up Castle Hill and over the
turrets of the Henry VIII Gate.

This, Fitzherbert's second flight, was
altogether a much more successful effort.
Even so, he tired rapidly, and, seeing a

square of grass in an inner courtyard, he
landed thankfully upon it. It was a crash-
landing that knocked the wind out of
him, and for some time he lay and
gasped for breath.

Finally recovered, he looked about
him. Then he saw a movement at an
upper window. Someone was looking
down at him. He could not see the figure
clearly, but it appeared to be dressed in
black!

If that's the Queen, thought Fitzherbert, I'd better make myself comfortable before I meet her. He stood up and suited his actions to his words.

"That's better!" he said, and he waddled off slowly towards the nearest door.

The Lady of the Bedchamber lost no time in contacting the Lord Steward of Her Majesty's Household.

"There's a large bird," she said to him, "in the Queen's private courtyard, and she wants it removed immediately."

"What sort of a bird?" asked the Lord Steward.

"I don't know," said the Lady of the Bedchamber. "It was something like a swan. But, then again, it was something like a goose."

The Lord Steward of Her Majesty's

Household sent for the Ornithologist Royal, the man who looked after the Queen's birds.

"There's a large bird," he said, "in Her Majesty's private courtyard. Get rid of it, will you?"

"What sort of a bird?" asked the Ornithologist Royal.

"Part swan, part goose, apparently."

"Part swan, part goose!" murmured the Ornithologist Royal excitedly to himself as he hurried to do the Lord Steward's bidding. "Could it be . . . ? Could it be?"

When the door into the courtyard opened, Fitzherbert was disappointed to see a man emerge. He seemed a nice man, however, for he produced some pieces of bread which he offered to the swoose. But no sooner had Fitzherbert begun to eat them than he was grabbed, his wings pinioned to his sides, and he was carried, kicking and struggling, away.

"It is! It is!" said the Ornithologist Royal as he listened to his captive's cries of protest, a blend of the grunting bark of an angry swan and the cackling of an outraged goose. He carried Fitzherbert to the Royal Menagerie, where all manner

of creatures were housed, presented as gifts to the Queen by visiting foreign rulers.

"It is!" said the Ornithologist Royal again as he feasted his eyes upon Fitzherbert, now shut in a large cage. "I had heard tales of such a bird, but never thought to see one! It is a swoose!"

"That bird," said the Lord Steward of Her Majesty's Household later. "Have you dealt with it?"

"Yes," said the Ornithologist Royal.

"What was it?"

"It is a swoose!" said the Ornithologist Royal. "A cross between a swan and a goose! A *rara avis* indeed! Her Majesty should be told."

The Lord Steward of Her Majesty's Household remembered enough of his Latin to say to the Lady of the

Bedchamber, "It's a rare bird, the one that was in the Queen's courtyard. Called a swoose apparently. Her Majesty should be told."

Nervously, for the Queen did not like to be told things, preferring that people should not speak until they were spoken to, the Lady of the Bedchamber approached her sovereign.

"Forgive me, Your Majesty," she said, "but that bird, that you saw earlier this morning . . ."

"Well?" said the Queen, her face set in its usual grim mode.

"I am given to understand, ma'am, that it is a swoose."

"A what?"

"A swoose, ma'am."

To the great astonishment of the Lady of the Bedchamber, something that might almost have been called a small

smile appeared on the Royal face. Never
in all the many years she had served at
court had the Lady of the Bedchamber
seen such a thing.

"A swoose," said Queen Victoria.
"Why, surely that must be part swan,
part goose!"

"Perhaps Your Majesty might care to

see the creature?" said the Lady of the Bedchamber.

"We would," said the Queen.

So it was that Fitzherbert, puzzled and angry at being shut in, saw the doors of the Royal Menagerie opened by a pair of bewigged footmen and a procession enter.

Followed by the Lord Steward, the Ornithologist Royal and the Lady of the

Bedchamber, and attended by the Lord
Chamberlain, the Comptroller of Her
Majesty's Household, the Master of the
Horse and several Ladies-in-Waiting,
came a short dumpy figure, dressed all in
black.

For some time Queen Victoria stared at
Fitzherbert without speaking. Naturally
no one else spoke.

Then the Queen said, "Are we right?

Is this bird indeed half-swan and half-goose?"

"Your Majesty is perfectly correct," said the Ornithologist Royal.

"And it is a rarity?"

"Indeed, ma'am."

"We do not like to see it so imprisoned. Open the door of its cage."

"But, ma'am . . ." began the
Ornithologist Royal, fearing that the bird
might misbehave itself in some way,
might even (dreadful thought) peck the
Royal ankles.

"Do as we say," snapped the Queen,
"and look sharp about it," and the
Ornithologist Royal looked very sharp
indeed.

Fitzherbert could, of course,
understand nothing of the medley of
sounds that the humans made.
However, it was clear to him that, thanks
to the Queen, he was to be a prisoner no
longer, and he thought that he should
show his gratitude.

With measured tread he walked out of
the cage and stood at attention before the

Queen. Then he slowly uncurled his long neck and laid his head upon the ground at the very feet of the monarch in a gesture that was the nearest he could come to a courtly bow.

To the amazement of the Lord Steward of Her Majesty's Household and the Ornithologist Royal and the Lady of the Bedchamber and the Lord Chamberlain and the Comptroller of Her Majesty's Household and the Master of the Horse and the Ladies-in-Waiting and the two bewigged footmen, none of whom recalled ever seeing such a sight before, Queen Victoria looked down at the swoose and smiled broadly.

"We are amused," said the Widow of Windsor.

4.

The news that something had made the
Queen smile for the first time in a quarter
of a century, or, in other words, since the
death of her husband Prince Albert,
spread like wildfire among the courtiers
at Windsor Castle. Not only had she
smiled once, but had continued to do so,
and had even spoken quite pleasantly to
a number of people. More, she had
exchanged her widow's cap of black for
one of white lace, and all because of that
swoose!

"It's all so beautifully timed," the Lord
Steward of Her Majesty's Household said
to the Lady of the Bedchamber. "Next
year it's the Queen's Golden Jubilee as
you know, when the whole kingdom will
be celebrating her fifty years on the

throne, and she will have to go about and show herself to the people. How pleased they will be to see her wearing a happy face again after all those years of gloom. The greatest care must be taken of that bird."

Unfortunately, it wasn't.

The very next morning, the Ornithologist Royal came in armed with a large pair of scissors. He intended to clip the flight feathers of one of the swoose's wings, a painless operation which would render the bird incapable of flight. Little did he guess that Fitzherbert had plans of his own.

First, despite having been released from his cage the previous evening on the Queen's orders, he had been shut up again as soon as she had gone, and this he did not like.

Second, he was longing to tell the

water-vole all about his audience with
Queen Victoria.

So the moment the Ornithologist Royal
opened the cage, Fitzherbert pushed past
him and made his way as fast as he could
along a corridor and out through a door.

"Stop! Stop!" cried the Ornithologist Royal, hurrying after him, scissors in hand, and then could only stand and watch in horror as the swoose took wing and flew away towards the Thames.

Fitzherbert flew upriver, trying to remember whereabouts it was that he had met the vole, when suddenly he saw him swimming across a little backwater.

"Alph!" he cried, and swooping down, landed with a great splash. He looked around, but could only see a couple of moorhens that squawked angrily at him from the rushes.

Then he saw a blunt brown head break surface.

"Alph!" he cried again. "Remember me?"

"How could I forget you?" said the vole sharply. "First time we met, you nearly ran me down, and now you drop

out of the sky almost on top of me.
You're a clumsy great hummock and no
mistake."

"Sorry, Alph," said Fitzherbert. "I was
in a hurry to tell you. I've seen the
Queen! And what d'you think – she
smiled at me!"

"Fancy!" said Alph.

He swam to the bank, and climbed out
and shook himself.

"Wonder why?" he said.

"I don't really know," said Fitzherbert. "She seemed to like me. And they were all very pleased. Everyone was ever so nice to me."

"They didn't shut you up then?" said Alph.

"Well, yes, they did, but I escaped."

"What for?"

"Why, to come and find you and thank you."

"What for?"

"For suggesting I should visit the Queen. It was a great idea. I must be getting back now, I dare say Her Majesty's missing me, wouldn't you think?"

For a moment the water-vole did not answer. He sat on his haunches, combing his very small round ears with his forepaws. Then he fixed his very small beady eyes on the swoose.

"I hope you know what you're doing, young fellow," he said. "It's all very well being the Queen's pet, but what if she gets fed up with you, eh?"

'Well, then I suppose she'd just let me go."

4

"She might," said Alph. "Or she might not. There's plenty of meat on you from what I can see. You don't want to end up like that, do you?"

"End up like what?" asked Fitzherbert.

"Eaten," said Alph. "At Windsor," and down his burrow he went.

5.

Meanwhile, back at the castle, panic reigned.

Everyone now knew that the swoose had flown away. Everyone, that is, except the Queen, and all were waiting, horrified, for the moment when she would find out.

The Ornithologist Royal in particular was in a cold sweat. He had let the bird escape. He, everyone agreed, would lose his job.

So it was with a great sigh of relief that the worried man saw Fitzherbert come winging back over the battlements to land once more in the inner courtyard. Armed with his scissors, he hurried out.

As he did so, an upper window was flung open and a commanding voice

called out, "Stop! And wait for us!"

The Ornithologist Royal stopped and waited, his heart in his mouth. What if the bird should take off again?

But Fitzherbert had no intention of doing so. To begin with, the flight to Alph and back had been quite tiring, and secondly, though he did not understand the words, he recognized the note of command in the Royal tones.

In a little while Queen Victoria emerged from a side door into the courtyard, leaning upon the arm of the Lady of the Bedchamber.

The Ornithologist Royal was a tall man, but he felt very small at sight of the dumpy little Queen's frowning face.

"What," she said, "are you doing with those scissors?"

"If you please, Your Majesty," said the Ornithologist Royal, "I was intending to pinion the bird."

"To pinion it?"

"To cut the flight feathers of one wing, ma'am."

"With what object?"

"To prevent the bird from leaving you."

"Leaving *us*?" said the Queen. "Flying away, from *our* presence, do you mean? What an absurd idea! You will put those scissors away, sir, or it will be you who is leaving."

Soon the whole court knew that, far from being chopped off, the feathers of the Queen's pet swoose must on no account

be so much as ruffled. He was to have the choicest food, such as fresh young vegetables from the kitchen gardens, brought to him by the Royal Head Gardener in person, and Scotch oatmeal porridge served by the Queen's manservant, John Brown.

In addition, the Royal Head Gardener's little daughter was appointed Swoosegirl-in-Waiting, to take Fitzherbert for daily walks in Windsor Great Park. By night, however, he was still shut in the Royal Menagerie for his own safety (for foxes, the Ornithologist Royal was sure, would be no respecters of sweese), but the Queen came in each evening to see her pet. Fitzherbert would make his bow, the Queen would smile, and everyone would heave a sigh of relief at the welcome change that had come over the crusty old lady.

At first Fitzherbert found the nights
trying. By day there were so many
people making a fuss of him, but at night
he was lonely. None of the other inmates
of the menagerie such as parrots or
monkeys bothered to talk to him, and he

thought how nice it would be to have a chat with someone like Alph.

How pleasant it was then to hear a friendly voice one evening, just after the Queen and her company had left.

A cultured voice it was, a little singsong in tone, and altogether quite unlike the country voice of the water-vole, though in fact it belonged to another rodent.

"How are you settling in, may one ask?" said the voice, and Fitzherbert looked up to see that the speaker was a rat.

He had come across rats before, in the farmyard, ugly-looking creatures with rough brown coats, but this one was quite different.

To begin with, it was smaller and slenderer than a farm rat, with large thin ears and the longest of tails, longer even than its whole body. And second, that body was clothed in the glossiest of blue-black fur.

Altogether it was the most elegant animal, Fitzherbert thought, and he answered politely, "Quite well, thank you."

"Allow me to introduce myself," said the black rat. "My name is Maharanee."

"Fitzherbert," said the swoose.

"A noble-sounding name," said Maharanee.

"So's yours," said Fitzherbert. "It sounds foreign."

"So it is," said the black rat. "Her Majesty, as you may know, is also Empress of India, and her loyal subjects within the raj often send her gifts of animals. I stowed away with such a shipload, believing my proper place to be at court."

"I don't quite understand," said Fitzherbert.

"I myself am of Royal blood. I was born in a palace, so it is fitting that I should associate myself with Her Majesty. Maharanee, you see, means 'Great Queen'."

"Oh," said Fitzherbert. "So you're a favourite of hers too, are you?"

"I wouldn't exactly say that," replied Maharanee. "The English, you know, are less than friendly towards our brown cousins and are apt to tar black rats with the same brush. I tend therefore to keep a low profile. But you certainly seem to have taken Her Majesty's fancy. You're quite the Royal pet."

Until she gets fed up with me, thought Fitzherbert, and then suddenly remembered that that was what Alph had said.

"Look here, Maharanee," he said. "You don't suppose she'd ever . . . eat me, do you?"

The black rat looked at the swoose consideringly, and strangely, she too echoed Alph's words.

"She might," she said. "Or she might not. But if you are ever to be on the menu, I shall hear about it. I spend a good deal of time in the castle kitchens. Rely upon me to give you warning, Fitzherbert my friend."

So the time passed pleasantly for the swoose. Not only did he enjoy the favour of the Queen, with all the benefits that came with it; but now he had two friends.

At night he had long and interesting conversations with the much-travelled Maharanee, and as often as he liked, he flew upriver for a chat with the homespun Alph. To see the swoose go gave the Ornithologist Royal fifty fits at first, but gradually he became confident that the bird would always return.

All went well until the Head Cook and Bottlewasher at Windsor Castle reached retirement age and was replaced.

The black rat arrived in Fitzherbert's cage one evening in high excitement.

"What do you think!" she said. "There is a French chef in the kitchen! No more stodgy, unimaginative English cooking. Now we shall see food fit for a Queen and leftovers fit for a Maharanee! There is nothing that a good chef cannot cook."

Except sweese, I hope, thought Fitzherbert.

6.

Soon after this, some foreign cousins of the Queen were due to stay at the castle, and the new chef was instructed to plan a modest ten-course dinner for the visitors.

"And make sure that the main course is something really spectacular, said the Lord Steward.

The French chef sought the advice of the Queen's Butler.

"Is there something," he asked, "that only Royalty may eat, *monsieur*?"

The Queen's Butler thought for a moment.

"Why yes," he said. "There is. Swan. Royal birds, swans are. No one else is allowed to eat them. There are plenty down there on the Thames."

Roast swan and all the trimmings, thought the chef. That will indeed be *spectaculaire*!

All might yet have been well had not the chef lost his way in the many halls and corridors of the castle. One morning he took from his knife-rack the largest of his carving knives, closely watched, though he did not know this, by an elegant blue-black creature crouching beneath a dresser.

He fingered the knife's edge, and then, shaking his head at its bluntness, set off to have it sharpened at the Armoury. However, he failed to understand the directions given him, and became confused in the maze of passages.

Opening a door, he found himself in an enclosed courtyard, in the centre of which was a perfect square of brilliantly green grass.

Right in the centre of it was a large shape.

The chef's hand tightened on his carving knife.

"*Voilà!*" he said softly. "No need to go to the river. The bird has come to me!"

Fitzherbert was dozing, a little tired after his daily walk. The Swoosegirl-in-Waiting had gone home to tea, and the Ornithologist Royal had not yet arrived to take the Queen's pet to the menagerie for the night.

Suddenly the swoose was woken by the voice of Maharanee.

"Fly, Fitzherbert, fly!" squealed the black rat.

Opening his eyes, the swoose saw a man approaching, a man dressed all in white and wearing a tall white hat, a man brandishing a huge knife!

At that very moment, a door opposite opened, and out of it, supported by her

Lady of the Bedchamber, came Queen Victoria.

In his terror, Fitzherbert totally disregarded Maharanee's instructions. Indeed, he completely forgot that he possessed his wild father's powers of flight and reverted to his mother's farmyard waddle.

Grunting, barking, cackling at the top of his voice, he hastened towards the Queen and turned and stood in front of her, his eyes fixed in horror on that dreadful knife that was destined, he was sure, for his throat.

Then, drawn by the terrible noise that the swoose was making, a host of people appeared and fell upon the wretched chef and dragged him away.

Later that evening, when all had been explained (and the luckless chef sent hurriedly back to France), the Queen came with her company into the menagerie. They brought a gilded chair for her, and she sat and looked at her swoose.

"What courage!" she said quietly. "Not only did he sound the alarm, but he stood before us, thinking that we were to be murdered. He believed that he was saving us!"

Everyone looked at everyone else, but nobody said anything.

"We shall reward him for his bravery," said the Queen, and those nearest could see that her old eyes were twinkling.

"Open the door of the cage," she commanded, and they opened it.

Fitzherbert stepped forward and stood at attention before the monarch's chair, and then, as always, lowered his head to the floor.

The Queen looked round at her courtiers and she positively grinned.

Then she raised her silver-headed, ebony walking-stick and with it she lightly touched Fitzherbert upon one shoulder.

"I dub thee Knight!" said Queen Victoria in a loud voice. "Arise, Sir Swoose!"

And slowly, proudly, to a burst of clapping from the smiling company of watchers, Fitzherbert arose.